ONCE UPON A TIME
AND
GRANDMA

OTHER BOOKS BY LENORE BLEGVAD

ANNA BANANA AND ME
illustrated by Erik Blegvad

RAINY DAY KATE
illustrated by Erik Blegvad

(McElderry Books)

ONCE UPON A TIME
AND
GRANDMA

written and illustrated by
LENORE BLEGVAD

MARGARET K. MCELDERRY BOOKS · New York

Maxwell Macmillan Canada · Toronto

Maxwell Macmillan International · New York · Oxford · Singapore · Sydney

For all my grandchildren

Margaret K. McElderry Books, Macmillan Publishing Company, 866 Third Avenue, New York, NY 10022
Maxwell Macmillan Canada, Inc., 1200 Eglinton Avenue East, Suite 200, Don Mills, Ontario M3C 3N1
Macmillan Publishing Company is part of the Maxwell Communication Group of Companies.

FIRST EDITION

Printed in Hong Kong by South China Printing Company (1988) Ltd.

The text of this book is set in Goudy Oldstyle. The illustrations are rendered in watercolor and pencil.
2   4   6   8   10   9   7   5   3   1

Library of Congress Cataloging-in-Publication Data
Blegvad, Lenore.   Once upon a time and Grandma / Lenore Blegvad. — 1st ed.   p.   cm.
Summary: When her grandchildren come for a visit, Grandma shows them the apartment where she lived
and tells them what she did when she was a young girl.
ISBN 0-689-50548-5
[1. Grandmothers—Fiction.   2. City and town life—Fiction.]   I. Title.
PZ7.B6180n   1993   [E]—dc20   92-7407

EMMA and her little brother Luke are visiting Grandma.
Every day Grandma takes them somewhere special.
Today she takes them to see a house.
Grandma says it's the house she used to live in, once upon a time.

High up on the fifth floor, they
can see Grandma's window.
They can see her fire escape.

But Grandma says she wasn't
Grandma when she lived there.
"Who were you?" Emma asks.

Grandma says she was a little girl called Norrie!
A little girl called Norrie?
Emma knows if Grandma says so, it must be true.
So she tries to believe her.
She listens to the things Grandma tells them....

When Grandma was a little girl
called Norrie, she used to look out
of that window way up there.
She watched the people
walking down here
in the street.
She watched the rain.

She watched the snow.
She was even watching when
these big trees were planted!

Grandma looks up at the leaves and smiles.
"They were little trees then," she says.

When Grandma was a little girl called Norrie,
she practiced the piano up there on the fifth floor.

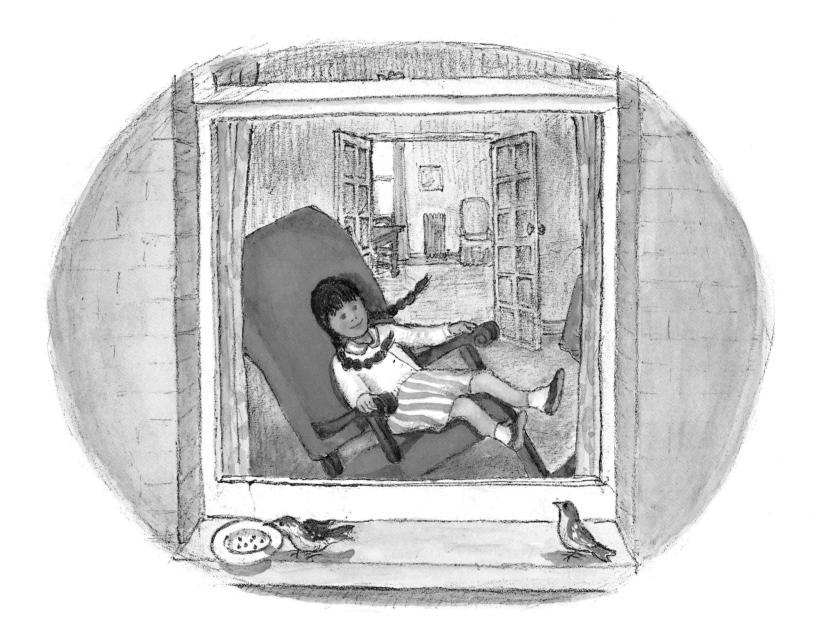

She used to rock in a big rocking chair by that window.

In the springtime, she would sit outside on the fire escape and blow soap bubbles!

"Outside, way up there?" Emma asks.
That little girl was lucky, she thinks.
Luke and I aren't allowed to do things like that.
Grandma just smiles. She has more to tell them.

When Grandma was a little girl called Norrie, an organ grinder used to play music down here in the street.

He had a tiny monkey on a string.

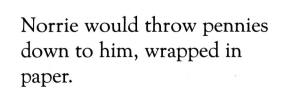

Norrie would throw pennies down to him, wrapped in paper.

The monkey would pick them up and wave his little hat.

Sometimes the old-clothes
man with a big bag on his
back would come by.

"I BUY OLD CLO-OOTHES!"
he would shout up
at the windows.
"I BUY OLD RAGS!"

And every day the iceman and the milkman would park their wagons right there.

And their great big horses too!

Sometimes the iceman would give Norrie little pieces of ice to suck on.

And sometimes Norrie would feed lumps of sugar to the big horses, right out of her hand!

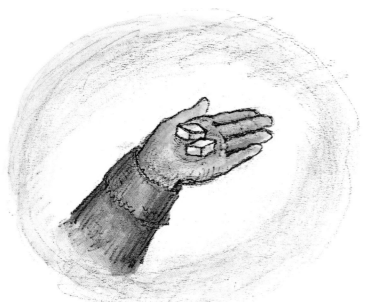

"Big, *big* horses?" Luke asks.

That little girl was brave, Emma thinks. Luke and I would be afraid to do that.

Grandma smiles. She has more to tell them.

Every winter, when Grandma was a little girl called Norrie, she built a snowman just where they are standing now.

In summertime, she played hopscotch
right there with her friends.
She jumped rope.
She played cowboys, sitting on that
railing.
And, Grandma says, she tap-danced in
that alleyway!

"Tap-danced!" Emma says to herself and
nudges her little brother.
That doesn't sound like Grandma at all.
But Grandma hasn't finished yet.

When she was a little girl
called Norrie, she had a turtle
up there in her room.

She had a paint box.

She had a little, tiny tea set,
with teeny-weeny flowers
painted on it.

In the summer, Grandma says, Norrie's house smelled of tar.
All the rugs were wrapped in tar paper to keep out the moths.
Norrie helped her daddy to tie the rugs up.

In the winter the rugs would be put down again.
The warm radiators would gurgle.
Norrie would eat alphabet soup from a big bowl.

And every night at bedtime, her daddy would read to her.

Once in a while, in the middle of the night,
Norrie would wake up and feel lonely.
Her room would be dark.
The long hall outside her door would be dark, too.
Very dark and very quiet.
Then Norrie would take a deep breath and call—
"MOM-M-M-M-M-M-Y!" as loud as she could.
"MOM-M-M-M-M-M-Y!"

And her mommy would come, barefoot and in her long
nightgown, to lie on the end of Norrie's bed, so Norrie wouldn't
feel lonely anymore.

That is what Grandma tells them.
She says she lived there when she was a
little girl and she did all those things,
once-upon-a-long-long-time ago.

Emma tries hard to imagine Grandma as
the little girl called Norrie.
But she can't.
Grandma is...Grandma.
She has always been Grandma.

Now Grandma smiles down at Emma
and Luke.

She takes a little box out of her purse.
"Don't you believe me?" she asks. "Then
look in here. What do you see?"

Emma and Luke look in the box.
Inside is a tiny tea set, with teeny-weeny
flowers painted on it.

"Is that Norrie's?" Luke asks.

"And if you still don't believe me," Grandma
says, "look at this. What does it say?"
She points to a word carved on the tree trunk
behind them.

"It says *Norrie!*" Emma reads in surprise.
"It does?" says Luke.
"My daddy put that there," Grandma says,
"when the tree and I were little. Now do you
believe me?"

Emma thinks about it.
She thinks about the tea set and the name carved
on the tree.

But it's not enough.
There's something else she has to know,
something else she has to ask.

"Grandma," Emma says at last, "can you...
can you...Grandma, *can you tap-dance?*"

Grandma looks surprised.
Then she smiles the biggest smile of all.
"Watch me!" she says.

And suddenly, Grandma is tap-dancing!
And Grandma is singing, "East Side, West Side,
all around the town!"

Grandma is tap-dancing, in her long green coat,
there in the alleyway!

"Oh, Grandma!" cry Emma and Luke.
"Teach us how to do that!
Teach us how to tap-dance just like you did
when you were a little girl called Norrie! *Please?*"

And she does.